Hello, Reader!

We kick. We run.
We're having fun!

You, too, will have fun reading
about this soccer game!

To Rachel and Joey
— G.M.

Text copyright © 1994 by Grace Maccarone.
Illustrations copyright © 1994 by Meredith Johnson.
All rights reserved. Published by Scholastic Inc.
HELLO READER! and CARTWHEEL BOOKS
are registered trademarks of Scholastic Inc.

Library of Congress Cataloging-in-Publication Data

Maccarone, Grace.
    Soccer game!/ by Grace Maccarone : illustrated by Meredith Johnson.
        p.   cm. — (Hello reader)
    Summary: Brief rhyming text follows a group of children through some exciting plays during a soccer game.
    ISBN 0-590-90754-9
    [1.   Soccer — Fiction.   2.   Stories in rhyme.]   I. Johnson, Meredith, ill.   II. Title.   III. Series.
    PZ8.3.M127So   1994
[E] —dc20
                                                                                    93-43742
                                                                                        CIP
                                                                                        AC
21 20 19 18 17 16 15   6 7 8 9/9

                            Printed in the U.S.A.   23

                    First Scholastic printing, August 1994

SOCCER GAME!

by Grace Maccarone
Illustrated by Meredith Johnson

SCHOLASTIC INC. Cartwheel B·O·O·K·S®
New York Toronto London Auckland Sydney

We start the game.

We're ready.

We aim.

We pass.

We fall.

They get the ball.

Away they go!

We're doomed!
Oh, no!

It's in the air.

Our goalie is there!

We dribble.

We pass.

We slip
on the grass.

We kick. We run.

We're having fun!

We see a hole.

We run to the goal.

The ball goes in.

Hooray! We win!